Gerard Melia
Edited by Josie Levine

This story is based on a disaster that actually
happened. Silvertown was devastated by an
explosion that occurred at 7 pm on Friday 19th
January 1917. All the characters in the story are
made up.

Longman

LONGMAN GROUP LIMITED
Longman House
Burnt Mill, Harlow, Essex CM20 2JE, England

First published 1984
ISBN 0 582 20167 5

Set in 12/15pt Times New Roman, Monophoto

*Printed in Hong Kong
by Wilture Printing Co., Ltd.*

Acknowledgements

We are grateful to the Imperial War Museum for permission
to reproduce the photograph on page 23, and to the
Newham Library Service for the photographs on pages 38,
41, 43, 46 and the cover.

1

It was Tuesday, December 12th, nearly five o'clock in the evening, when Mena and June strolled down Mochett Hill towards the centre of town. Normally, Tracey would have been with them, but that day she had dashed off straight after school to meet her parents at the town hall. They were going to buy her a new badminton racquet.

Tracey was good at sport. She was already captain of the school netball team, and now they had started up a badminton team as well, she had been made captain of that, too. To celebrate, Jane and Mena had bought her a smashing pair of socks to play in. They were emerald green with white stripes, and on each stripe there was a row of scarlet pimpernels.

Of course, Tracey could not wait until the first match to wear them, and she had gone to meet her mum and dad in them.

Christmas decorations twinkled in the sweetshop window, as Mena and Jane joined the number 27 bus queue. They were behind an old lady with two carrier bags, a tall, middle-aged man wearing a duffle coat and a young boy with a sliced loaf under his arm.

A 27 bus appeared at the top of the hill, and came down the road towards them. The man in the duffle coat signalled the driver to stop. Jane was looking out for the driver. Her Uncle Bill was a bus driver, and he worked the 27 route.

This driver was a stranger, though – a frightened stranger, struggling with the steering wheel. The bus was going all over the place. It veered towards them. Instinctively, they all jumped away from the edge of the pavement but the driver, managing to control the direction of the vehicle, steered it past them.

At the bus-stop the gradient of the hill increased. The bus moved faster. It was not a mad runaway, but a quiet, relentless missile pointing straight at the town. The driver, his foot brakes useless, must have been applying his handbrake desperately, for the smell of burnt rubber followed the vehicle downhill.

There was a boy from their school on the top deck waving mockingly at the girls. He thought the bus had passed them because it was full. Mena looked down the hill. Mercifully, the road was clear of people. Both the girls could hear the bus conductor ringing the bell continuously. The vehicle shuddered as the driver tried once more to apply the handbrake, but the weight of the bus was too great, and it rumbled on.

The driver pressed on the horn, trying to warn traffic ahead of him. It sounded like the death squeal of a dying animal. At the traffic lights there was a car. Like a bull with its head down, the bus rammed the rear of the car and catapulted it, bonnet first, into the window of the furniture shop on the corner of the crossroads. Then, trying vainly to control his rampant vehicle, the bus driver steered it towards the centre of the road and crunched the yellow lit bollards beneath its front axle. The bus wobbled as it digested the metal bollards. Then it came to a halt, broadside across the road.

Mena and Jane ran down the hill. Stunned and shocked, passengers stumbled drunkenly from the bus, and pedestrians stood staring at the chaos. For a moment, everything was held still. Then, a sound, a moan from the car, brought the tableau into action. A policeman appeared, and contacted his headquarters and the emergency service on his two-way radio. The man in the duffle coat ran past the girls and jumped through the shattered shop window. He tried to open the car door. It was locked. Reaching through a broken side window, he pulled the inside catch. As the door opened, a carrycot with a baby in it slid to the ground.

Mena pushed past the watching crowd, and gently lifted the carrycot. She looked at Jane who pointed at a three-piece suite that had been pushed against the rear wall of the shop. They put the carrycot on the settee. Mena removed the shawl to inspect the baby. It was fast asleep.

The policeman and the man in the duffle coat levered the driver of the car – the baby's mother – from behind the steering wheel. Blood striped her face from a broad gash in her forehead. She was unconscious. The two men lowered her gently to the floor, and covered her with their coats.

The young boy with the loaf appeared. Seeing Mena and Jane, he came through the shop window and sat on the settee with them. He had broken the wrapping round the loaf and was eating the crust. He stopped nibbling and tugged at Jane's sleeve.

'Hey, girl! Hey, girl!' he said.

'What do you want? You shouldn't be here, you know.'

'You'd better tell them ... tell the policeman ...'

4

'Tell him what?'

'Tell him there's somebody under the car. There's some legs sticking out.'

He pulled Jane's arm again. She stood up and took a couple of steps towards the car. By now there was a nightmare of noise from the arrival of the ambulance, the fire engine and the police. The revolving yellow and blue lights reflected from the mirrors of the bedroom furniture in the damaged shop. Jane put her hand on the crunched car boot, and bent forward. There, as the boy had said, sticking out from the rear of the car, was a pair of legs – a pair of legs clad in emerald green socks with white stripes and a row of scarlet pimpernels.

It was Tracey, and she was dead.

2

Mrs Thomas stood in the pale winter sunshine, smiling towards the school garden. The garden was now in its third year, and the shrubs and plants had settled and roamed a little, giving it a disorganised but natural appearance. It pleased her to think that it had once been a corner of the tarmaced playground. She hoped that when the next generation of pupils came to the school they would use and look after it with the same respect as the pupils who had designed and created it.

It had been an excellent project. The work had gone well at the time, and was paying off now. Not only had the boys and girls who had done the work planted evergreen shrubs, but they had made sure that there was colour in the garden throughout the year. Now, as January shaded into February, the small, yellow aconites were being joined by crocuses and snowdrops.

Mrs Thomas scanned the bright little flower

blooms once more and spotted a patch of broken stems. She sighed. Billy Taplow had visited the garden again. Billy was seventeen, an ex-pupil and, like many other young men in Stratford Park, was currently unemployed. He liked to pick a few flowers to take to his girl-friend who worked at the Old Folks' Home – or so the Deputy Head had reported.

'If I actually catch him, he'll regret the encounter,' Mrs Thomas said to herself.

Deep in thoughts of retribution, she hardly noticed Mena enter the garden and sit on one of the benches. But when she saw Jane follow her there, she forgot Taplow and what she would do to him if she caught him. Mrs Thomas had worked hard in the hope that Jane and Mena would be able to continue as friends. It was necessary work, for after Tracey's death they had found each other's company profoundly unsettling. Every time they met they had cried, each reminding the other of their mutual loss. Mrs Thomas thanked God for the Christmas holiday when they were not forced to see each other every day. It was good to see that, some four weeks after the start of the new term, they had got back together again. Even better to know that they had managed to do so over their work, and that this work was their way of remembering Tracey. Yes, Mrs Thomas was quietly pleased with her efforts to help the girls readjust to school life.

When she had begun talking with them, Mena had suggested making a memorial as a way of facing school life without their friend.

'You don't mean a gravestone, do you?' Jane had said.

'Of course not,' Mena had snapped impatiently. 'I mean we ought to do something as a lasting memory of her – something here in school.'

Jane had suggested that perhaps a corner of the garden could be called after her, and some seats put there with her name on them. Mrs Thomas had liked the idea, and thought it would be right for the whole school to contribute. Mena and Jane agreed, but it still did not seem enough for the two special friends. They wanted to do something more, and, in any case, a garden in their part of London might not last.

'We've no guarantee the garden or the school will be here in ten years' time,' Mena said. 'Look how they've pulled down whole streets around here in the last few years, and now they're closing schools. They might bulldoze the school and the garden, and then our friend would be forgotten altogether. No, I want to do something more than make a corner of the garden here.'

Mrs Thomas had gone ahead with the garden idea on behalf of the whole school, but Jane and Mena had not had any other ideas for themselves until Mena had to find a subject for her CSE history project. Then she remembered that Tracey had started her project earlier in the year because of her sports commitments. Mena remembered that Tracey had gone to the library to the local history section and had found the diary of a young girl among the documents that the library had collected. It was the diary of a girl who had been killed in the Silvertown explosion of 1917.

'That's it!' Mena had said to Jane. 'That's it! Let's finish our friend's project for her. A joint project . . . you and me. Come on! Let's go and ask Mrs Thomas if we can.'

Of course, the girls had no trouble in persuading Mrs Thomas. She had readily agreed, and Jane – not all that given to school work – had been swept along on the tide of enthusiasm. This was different, anyway. It was for Tracey.

Mrs Thomas watched the girls now as they sat on the seat, then she ambled towards them.

'Am I interrupting, my dears,' she said,

announcing her presence.

Jane and Mena stood up immediately.

'Do sit down. I'll sit with you, if I may, unless you are discussing a private matter.'

'No, Madam,' Jane replied. 'We're just trying to decide how to divide the work on Tracey's Memorial.'

'And what have you decided?'

'Nothing yet, Madam,' Mena told her. 'We don't know how big the job is. So we're going to see Mr Watkins to find out.'

'Mr Watkins is the local history librarian, Madam,' Jane broke in. 'He's terrific ... he looks exactly like ...'

'He says we can go down to the library this afternoon, Madam,' Mena said.

Mrs Thomas laughed to herself.

'Are you sure you are going to see this thing through, Jane?' she asked.

Jane nodded.

'I hope this is the new dawn you promised me, Jane. Many of your previous dawns have developed into rather dull, damp disappointments, my girl. A good history project will pull your course work up considerably, and give you confidence for the exams.'

'Yes, Madam,' Jane said, attempting to

muster an I'm-trying-my-best look.

She smiled. Mrs Thomas smiled. Mena smiled. They all smiled at each other. They remained smiling, and embarrassed. None of them knew why they were smiling. Mrs Thomas and Mena looked at Jane. She had started it. Jane looked at the floor.

'Haven't you two gone yet?'

It was Mr Harding, the girls' form teacher, who got them out of their difficulty.

'Mr Watkins has gone to a lot of trouble finding special materials for you two. Now get over there, and remember, Jane, no tricks. I'll be phoning him later to see how you've been getting on.'

The girls got up to go, glad to be released from their headmistress's company. Mr Harding handed Mrs Thomas a note which she read as they made their way to the school gate. They could hear the headmistress's voice wafting over the garden.

'There are some flowers missing today, Mr Harding. Taplow is likely to be responsible, I think.'

Jane chuckled and linked arms with Mena.

'Good old Billy, he's been at it again,' she said.

'At what? What's he been up to?'

11

Mena never knew as much of the local gossip as Jane.

'He's nicked some crocuses and things and taken them to his girl-friend. You want to see her. She's old enough to be his mother.'

3

This was the girls' first visit to the reference library. When they had gone to the library before, they had seen the big, old-fashioned glass doors with the words REFERENCE LIBRARY set in the glass, but they had never been in.

Behind the doors, they found a young man working behind a desk. He was looking things up in a file. At the front of his desk, there was a stand-up label that said RECEPTION.

Jane handed him the letter from Mr Harding.

'We're from Stratford Park School,' she said. 'Our teacher arranged for us to see Mr Watkins.'

The librarian took the letter, picked up the phone and started to dial an extension number.

'Just a minute, please. I'll tell him you're here. Oh, Mr Watkins, there are two youngsters here from Stratford Park School . . . yes . . . OK . . . I'll tell them.'

He put down the receiver and pointed at some chairs on the other side of the small room.

'Mr Watkins will be along in a minute. He just needs to finish getting out the things that you need.'

The girls sat down in silence. Mena put her bag down between them. In it was Tracey's folder. It was a serious moment. They both felt excited and sad, at the same time, as they thought about their dead friend and the work they were proposing to do.

The previous night, Mena had looked through Tracey's folder, and earlier that day she and Jane had gone through it together. There was such a lot they did not know. Who was the girl whose diary Tracey had found? She had written her name all over the page, practising her signature, just like she, Mena, had done herself when she had been in the second year. How had the explosion happened in Silvertown in the first place? Would they ever be able to find out, or was this a wild goose chase? Well that's what Mr Watkins is for, Mena thought to herself.

At that moment, he came into the room.

'Jane? Mena?' he said.

The girls were surprised that he had remembered their names.

14

'Yes ... yes,' Jane said, thinking, as she looked at him, that it was going to be doubly worth doing the History Project. 'I'm Jane Anders and this is Mena ...'

'Mena Kaur Sandhu,' Mena smiled, apprehensively.

Mr Watkins was as good-looking as they remembered and it was having different effects on them both.

'Come this way, girls. I'll show you the materials we have, then you can decide how you want to work with them.'

They followed Mr Watkins into another room which was filled with books, old newspapers, pamphlets, posters, picture postcards, boxes which they later found had letters in them, and diaries left by local people of the past. On the walls, there were posters and enlarged photos of cuttings from old newspapers.

Mr Watkins waved an arm at everything in the room. From the way he spoke, the girls could tell that he was really keen on his work.

'History isn't just about kings and queens, you know. Every area has its history, and we're no exception here in Silvertown. Your friend Tracey had started work on one of the most spectacular aspects of our history. You see,

15

right here in Silvertown, during the First World War, there was a factory – the Bruner Mond factory – where they made explosives to use in the war, and we know that many local women worked there. When Tracey came down here to start her project she got interested in that newspaper cutting over there on the wall. You see ... the one about the Silvertown explosion on 19th January 1917 ...'

The girls walked over to read it. It was difficult. All the sentences were long and the language sounded strange – not like the way newspapers are written today. But they were able to find out enough to feel as interested as Tracey must have been.

They had been making explosives for the war over in France at the factory – when suddenly the whole dangerous business went wrong. Whose fault was it? Was enough care taken over the safety of the factory workers? The devastation was enormous, as if Silvertown itself had been the scene of one of the hideous battles of the war.

'When Tracey started her research,' Mr Watkins told the girls, 'she found this page of writing. You've seen the copy she made of it already ... a loose page from a girl's diary. If you go over there to that brown box marked

"Silvertown" you'll be able to see the original. I'll leave you with it. Then you can pull out the Silvertown file and begin your research. I'll be over there at my desk. If you need any help, don't shout, just walk across and ask. OK?'

The girls nodded enthusiastically, and set to work. Mena found a faded yellow page in the Silvertown box and placed it on the desk between herself and Jane. They began to read.

March 12th 1916

This morning Emily Bridges from Custom House Road was killed at the Brunner Mond Factory where they make the explosives for shells. She was run over by a railway wagon. Mrs Bridges must be very sad. She lost her eldest son Peter last year in France and her youngest son Arthur came home two weeks ago having lost a leg in the war. Our Rosie started war work last week, but she is not able to tell me what she does because it is a secret and she is not allowed to say anything. My father and my brother Ken were up all night at a big fire in the City of London. It made me realise that their work in the Fire Brigade is as dangerous as fighting the war itself over in France. Mr Hodges, our teacher, had put me in for a scholarship at West Park Grammar School. Mrs Beckhost at No 19 has had a baby. I wonder if she wishes that she was back home in Belgium? That's all for today. God bless all the soldiers in France.

Winnie

Mena read the passage several times. How could someone get run over by a railway wagon at a factory, she wondered. Had the wounded soldier told the girl who wrote the diary about the war? Did she get her scholarship?

Mena crossed to Mr Watkins' desk and spoke to him.

'I'd like to know more about the girl who wrote the diary,' she said.

'So would I, Mena. But information like that has got to be dug out of our archives.'

Mr Watkins pointed at a pile of brown cardboard boxes.

'Do you think we might find the rest of her diary?' Mena asked.

'We have about five pages of it. The rest was burnt in the explosion.'

'Who was she?' Jane asked, as she joined Mena and Mr Watkins.

'Her full name was Winifred Alice Dibbs. She's buried with her father and brother in Gatworth Cemetery. They were killed as well, you know.'

'Will we be able to find out more about her?' Jane asked.

'Yes, but you'll have to be like detectives and hunt for clues. You could start with the newspapers. We've got copies of the *Stratford*

Park Gazette for every year since 1904. All the papers are on microfilm. I'll show you how to use the viewing machine so you can read them.'

Mr Watkins selected a roll of film on which there were photo negatives of each page of the *Stratford Park Gazette* for 1917, and put it in the machine. The viewer magnified each page, and the control knobs on either side of the machine were used for focusing on a particular part of a page, and for winding the microfilm on. When Mena started to use it, she felt as if she was peering into a time machine. There, in black and white, were the happenings of March 25th 1916.

Burglars' Dramatic Arrest

Followed by an account of how the police had arrested three Russian men boring a hole from a tea shop into the jeweller's shop next door. A Mr Charles Demsey of Albert Road, North Woolwich was charged with 'working a horse in an unfit state' and a drunken man fell off the roof of his house and killed a passing dog! There was a description of the Shakespeare Tercentenary celebrations, cricket and football scores and lists of those recently reported killed in France. The advertisements made Mena chuckle and she called Jane over to have a look at them. LW Spratt & Sons had taken a quarter page to advertise 'Kingsonia Natural Figure Corsets' (with the new locker hip). At the top of the advertisement it said – 'A word to all patriotic women: The unfailing patriotism of the British Woman is one of the outstanding features of the great war, but few women realise how important it is to the country that they insist upon having *British Goods*.' 'The World's Premier Contralto Dame Clara Butt – "I am extremely pleased with your Abdo Corsets. They give the required lines to the figure without cramping it or interfering in any way with *free breathing*."' Six ladies modelled in various styles of corsets available.

Mena and Jane laughed so much at the corsetted women that Mr Watkins had to remind them of the rule of silence in the reference library.

When Jane took over the controls of the viewing machine, Mr Watkins showed her the first button which speeded up the microfilm so that she did not have to go through a month's paper page-by-page. A week, a month could be skipped very easily.

Jane pressed the button and the time

machine sped forward to July 18th 1916.

'the arrest of Opium Smugglers – two Chinamen were caught carrying 3 lbs of opium in their belts as they entered the Royal Albert Dock. The sentence was six months' hard labour.'

Jane found the small ads very interesting too.

'Choice of two Welsh Mares, 14 hands, splendid workers £22' ...
'Smoked sausages $1\frac{1}{2}$ each' ...
'India Pale Ale No 3.3s 6d per doz' ...
'Glace kid Bar Shoes – 8/11' ...
'Dainty white voile blouse $4/11\frac{1}{2}$ JR Roberts Ltd, Broadway, Stratford Park'

Jane was enthralled by the style and elegance of the dresses and hats which could be bought at the store of JR Roberts.

'I wonder if that was a relative of our Mrs Roberts,' Jane muttered to herself.

The two girls continued to turn the control knob of the viewing machine and, occasionally forgetting the rule of silence, emitted exclamations of surprise and mirth at what seemed to them the oddities of the past. Mr Watkins wisely did not interfere.

Half an hour later the phone rang. It was

Mr Harding checking on the girls as he had promised.

'Apparently,' Mr Watkins told them, 'you are due back at school at 2.45. If you start now you'll just make it.'

'It's OK for two of us to work on the same thing, isn't it?'

'Of course, Jane. In fact, there's so much work in this project you'll need two of you to do it properly, anyway.'

Mena asked the next question.

'When can we start properly?'

'Tomorrow, if you wish. There's a lot to do. By the way, I came across something only yesterday which might be of use to you.'

Mr Watkins pulled a book out of the pile on his desk. It was called *Fourteen-Eighteen*, by John Masters. He turned to page ninety-nine and showed them a picture of Silvertown after the explosion.

On the page opposite the picture was a description of an explosion in an ammunition factory similar to that of Silvertown. Mr Watkins read to them from the eye-witness account.

'A dull flash, a sharp deafening roar and I felt myself being hurled through the air, falling down,

The remains of the Brunner Mond factory and its
surroundings after the explosion

down, down into darkness ... In the glare I saw girls shrieking with terror, their clothes alight, blood pouring from their wounds ... Swiftly, surely, the flames crept nearer. Something was lying across my legs. I could not rise. I tried desperately to free them, tugging at my left one, which appeared buried in a wet mass of blood and earth, it lifted easily in my hand, so easily, so light – My leg had been blown off and I held in my tortured hands the dripping thigh and knee ...'

Jane felt sick. The leg she saw in her imagination was wearing green skiing socks. Why had Mr Watson read that particular bit out to them? He had known Tracey, too. He must have known it would upset them for more than what was written – although that was bad enough.

4

Jane regarded herself as a tough girl and the fact that she had nearly fainted on hearing the description of the effects of an explosion made her very reticent in reporting the library visit to her classmates. Mena maintained a discreet silence about the matter. She wondered whether Jane would continue with the project now.

Walking home from school that day, Jane was abnormally quiet–so quiet that Mena had to initiate the conversation.

'Real war isn't very pleasant, is it?'

'You're right there, kiddo – it's not a bit like in the films on the tele. Do you know what's missing?'

Mena shook her head.

'Music. There's no background music in real-life war. When that woman had her leg blown off, there wasn't a big orchestra playing sad music. There was just her lying there on her own and her leg lying beside her . . . separate. I thought about it in bed last night.'

They walked on for a while in silence, which Jane eventually broke.

'I'd still like to know about it though, wouldn't you?'

'Yes. Yes, I would. Shall we go back to see Mr Watkins, like he suggested?' Mena asked.

'When? Do you mean now?'

'Yes, why not? There's nothing on the tele till *Crossroads*.'

Since school was just over for the day and kids from lots of schools were coming into the library, Mr Watkins was very busy, but the girls' interest had obviously been roused, and he did not intend to put them off now.

'Can we start by reading the girl's diary, please?' Mena asked.

'There's not a lot to look at. As I told you earlier. There are only five pages – discovered when the rubble of the house was being removed. Most of the paper had been burned.'

Mr. Watkins produced what had once been a blue school exercise book. It still retained its front cover, but the back had been ripped off, and there were scorch marks at the bottom of each remaining sheet of paper.

Monday 7th September 1916

Yesterday was Sunday. I went for a walk in the evening, after Sunday School, to the Woolwich Ferry. I pushed young Bert in his pram. It was so calm and quiet at first. Suddenly we heard thunder, or that's what we thought it was, but the sky was clear and full of red streaky clouds. We ran home just in case. All the street was talking about it. Mr Green, who works at the Town Hall in East Ham, told my dad it was the Germans and the French shelling each other in France. The Town Hall had been informed by the Government and Lloyd George that it was at a place called the Somme. I'm tired of this war. Pray God it will be over soon.

God Bless everyone.   Winnie

Wednesday 9th September 1916

The thing I think about most inside myself is the examination for the Girls' Grammar School. My teacher has put my name down for it, but I'm not sure I'm good enough. I don't want to look silly by getting the lowest marks in Silvertown. My teacher says I must practise writing letters, but I don't know anyone to write real letters to – not now our Lucy is coming back from America. I could write to Alfie, I suppose. I could explain what it was all about in my first letter. He is a boy in our class. He is very quiet and serious. I don't think he would laugh at me. I'll write my first letter tomorrow. He only lives three streets away, so I can walk round and put it through his door.

God Bless everyone.   Winnie

Sunday 13th September

I forgot to do my diary because our Lucy came back from America with my new brother-in-law, William. She met him out there in America but he came from Fulham in the first place. He has come back to join the army so she has come with him. We had a welcome home party, and that is why I forgot. Mrs Hopkins from No 9 next door, had another little girl yesterday. She is their sixth child. Mr Hopkins is a baker at the Millenium Mill. Mr Foster had another attack of his complaint. He calls it his 'Eastern-Ailment-Caught-While-Serving-the-Queen-in-South-Africa'. He used to be a soldier. My mother looks after him when he gets it bad and he can't get his breath. He lives on his own, next door to Mercer's shop.

God Bless Mr Foster and everyone.
Winnie

Monday 14th December

Although I only do my diary once a week now I'm very glad I've kept it up. It is nice to look back on things I'd forgot had happened a few months ago. Lucy now lives at No 1. William has joined the army but he paid a whole year's rent on No 1 with money he brought from America. Lucy has a bank account, too. She works at Brunner Mond. She has two lodgers, Louise and Mary. They work at Brunner Mond, too. Louise is a real case. She tells very funny stories about her aunt in Lancashire who breeds canaries. We are looking forward to

Christmas. Dad and our Ken were at another big fire in the East India Docks last night. Ken brought home a bag of Brazil nuts. Dad says we move into the Fire Station house across the road on Jan 2nd. All the firemen's houses are built with shinning red brick. The others have yellow brick fronts. I'm not . . .

The bottom of the page was torn. Mena felt a pang of disappointment, and Jane was annoyed.

'I can't stand it when you get cut off like that.'

'Perhaps she was going to say she wasn't keen on moving into one of the firemen's houses.'

'I suppose so. But it's not very satisfying is it?'

Jane stalked across to Mr Watkins.

'How can we find the end of this bit?' she asked abruptly.

He shook his head.

'Sorry Jane, I don't know for certain. I can only suggest possible ways of exploring the available information.'

'Well, what have you got? You're supposed to be helping us do this study . . . and the best bit is missing.'

Mr Watkins knew that they would be

delighted at school with the way Jane was getting involved in the project. He was delighted himself, so he checked any sharp response he might have made at another time to Jane's abrupt manner.

'Have you checked the newspapers yet? There's quite a lot there about the explosion,' he suggested.

'But that won't help to find the missing pages of the diary, will it?' Mena said, obviously sharing in Jane's frustration.

The trouble was that what they had read before, or seen on television had a beginning, a middle and an end. What happened next, and the ending, were essential to the enjoyment of the experience.

'Look girls,' Mr Watkins said, gently. 'In this kind of story you've got to put the pieces together like a jigsaw puzzle. The bits and pieces come from many different places. This room may not contain all the answers. You may have to look elsewhere'.

Jane could feel her enthusiasm for the project begin to drain away as he spoke, and even Mena, who always stuck with school work longer than Jane, was feeling disappointed. Mr Watkins tried to save the situation by suggesting something for them to do.

'As a beginning, look at the diaries and draw a map of the street. Then try to fit the families into the correct houses.'

'That's stupid,' Jane said, vehemently. 'How would we know who lived in Winnie's street?'

'I'll show you. You re-read all Winnie's diary papers and sketch what you find and I'll look up a map of the area for 1916.'

The girls laid the pages out side by side on a large table in the order they had read them. Mena took a piece of paper from her satchel and drew a street with a number of homes on each side. She numbered the houses 1–19 on one side and 2–20 on the other.

'The Belgian lady who had a baby lives in No 19,' Jane announced. 'Her name was Mrs Beckhost and Winnie lives in No 7.'

Mena filled in the names on her diagram. 'There's nothing on these next two pages about anyone living anywhere,' Jane said.

Mena checked. Jane was right, but there were references to the Woolwich Ferry as being within walking distance of Oldfield Road, and the boy Winnie thought she would write letters to lived three streets away. Mena made notes of this for later.

The next page said the Hopkins family lived

at No 9 and that Mr Foster lived on his own next to a shop. They didn't yet know where that was, so Mena made another note. The fifth page told them about Lucy going to live at No 1 and about the two lodgers. There were firemen's houses on the other side of the road.

When they had finished reading, Mena's sketch looked like this:

Firemen's houses

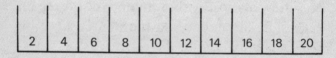

| 2 | 4 | 6 | 8 | 10 | 12 | 14 | 16 | 18 | 20 |

| 1 Lucy and 2 lodgers | 3 | 5 | 7 Winnie | 9 Hopkins family | 11 | 13 | 15 | 17 | 19 Mrs B the B |

They showed the diagram to Mr Watkins as he smoothed out the map of the area on the table.

'That's a good start,' he said. 'Now find Oldfield Street on the map and then draw the other streets and buildings around it. I'll find out about the firemen's houses from the Council Minutes, and we'll see if the Health Inspector reported on that shop. There's also a pile of rent books belonging to the Tatum Sugar Factory. Perhaps they owned a few houses in that street.'

The girls soon found Oldfield Street and they drew the map as Mr Watkins had suggested.

The rent books which Mr Watkins produced were very useful. By chance, five terraced houses in the street belonged to Tatum Sugar Refinery for use by their employees and the Health Inspector had made a report on a grocer's shop at No 2. The fireman's report stated that Silvertown Fire Station had a company of seven men and a senior Fire Officer, but it didn't say which houses they occupied.

Mena and Jane added in the names of the people they knew lived in Oldfield Street – Mercer's shop at No 2 and Mr Foster at No 4. They showed the map to Mr Watkins.

'Well done, girls. That's just what you need to start.'

'To start?' Jane exclaimed. 'I thought we were about to finish!'

'Really, Jane,' he said, reprovingly, 'now

Woolwich Ferry

River Thames

Ink Works

Dock

Brunner-Mond Factory

Petrol Tanks
Vesta Rubber Factory

Millenium Mills

Tatum Sugar Refinery

Dock Road

Mitter's Shop

Mr Foster

2 4 6 8 10 12

Fire Station

St Johns Church

14 16 18 20 22 24 26

Oldfield Street

1 3 5 7 9 11 13 15 17 19 21 23

Lucy and 2 lodgers

Winnie's family

Hopkins family

Mrs Beckhurst

Custom House Road

Sunday School

Silvertown School

you've got some idea of the area and the people, you can read the accounts of the story to see if they fit.'

'Well, of course, they'll fit. The people who were in the explosion were there so they're bound to be the same.'

She slapped her pencil noisily on the table. Mr Watkins can be a bit thick, she thought to herself.

'Most of the people who lived in Oldfield Road could have been killed,' said Mr Watkins patiently. 'They won't have told anybody anything. The accounts in the newspapers I've got here are written by people who weren't there at the time of the explosion.'

'Written by reporters you mean,' Mena said, brightly.

'Good, good, Mena. I can see you're getting the idea.'

Jane gave Mena a withering look. Mena went quiet.

Mr Watkins cast his eye over the map the girls had drawn. He checked the street names, the names of the church and the Sunday School, and the position of the factories along the river bank. It seemed accurate.

Taking their map, he led them into a side room which opened off the main room of the reference library. On a table he'd set out two books. They contained all the written accounts of the Silvertown Explosion of January 1917.

'Now girls, I want you to sit quietly and read, using the map to plot the explosion.'

Jane and Mena eagerly opened the first page. The style of writing was strange and old-fashioned, but the descriptions gripped their imaginations so that it was as if the walls of the room disappeared and they stood side by side with the writer in the desolation of Silvertown.

Language is inadequate to faithfully describe the scene of this great catastrophe. As I got to the heart of the area it seemed to me that the hand of a veritable titan had been at work. A titan with a lust for destruction. It was as if streets had never existed there before. Where previously a row of dwellings had stood there now remained a flattened heap of debris. Surrounding this scene of devastation were those houses, some 500 yards away, which now stood looking forlorn and dejected. A collection of dumb witnesses to the spectacle. In one street, lace curtains waved from windows at nobody, and the stairs rocked drunkenly in the gusts of wind that whistled inquisitively around the ruins on this cold January morning. The plaster had been scoured from the laths giving the rooms the appearance of a rib cage.

The Fire Station was demolished except for the

forty-foot tower they used for drying and testing the fire hose. The Brunner Mond factory site was as bare as a school playground with a huge hole in its centre marking the exact spot where the explosion had occurred. Hundreds of tons of earth had been ejected and spread in a thin layer, a mantle of death, upon the surrounding remains.

The explosion in its appalling and greedy intent had been indiscriminate in its destruction. A group of houses in the middle of Custom House Road remained standing – utterly alone, whilst a shop at the end of Oldfield Road was hardly damaged. Silvertown school, once a proud three-storey brick building, was reduced to rubble, but an adjacent wall was absolutely intact. A dozen chickens kept in boxes by the wall were untouched and they had laid six eggs the following morning which were taken to the soup kitchen at St John's Church down the road to help feed the survivors.

Someone had started a fire with rubbish and wood from the wrecked houses. A soldier and a clergyman stood warming themselves as I approached. The soldier had used the burning embers to brew a pot of tea. The red chapped fingers, cut and scarred by grappling with bricks and steel, peeped out of his mittens. Without a word being exchanged, he passed me an enamelled mug of hot tea. The clergyman gazed fixedly at the desolation around him. Yesterday he had a parish of lively, caring people. His parish had been emptied overnight.

'Just saying to the vicar,' the soldier said, 'them

'Just like the Somme this is' said the soldier as he spat in the fire. 'Just like the Battle of the Somme'

Sunday School kids were lucky . . . well perhaps not lucky, perhaps God was looking after 'em.'

'Which children?' I asked. The clergyman still remained staring at the destruction before him.

'That hall opposite the church over there – well it's not there now – you can see its roof lying flat in the roadway – it appears that the children and Sunday School teachers had finished their tea party – it was a kind of late Christmas party – and they were playing this singing game – Ring a Ring of Roses – when one of the helpers, a Miss Griffiths coming from the parsonage across the way sees this fire at Brunner Mond and she tells the Reverend here who was at the party.

'He went out to have a look and told everybody to keep calm. He'd hardly got the words out of his mouth when the explosion puts all the lights out and flings everybody to the ground. The building was made of corrugated iron lined with match-boarding and that somehow took the shock of the explosion. The glare from outside lit up the remains and seeing that the roof might totally collapse at any moment and bury the children, Miss Griffiths held up the lowest part of the roof on her back. Other helpers came to her assistance and whilst they were supporting the roof the children were taken out from underneath. Only three children were injured but they had trouble getting the roof struts off Miss Griffiths because they'd cut into her back.'

The soldier reached down and filled his mug with hot brown tea. He spaded five spoonfuls of sugar into it and stirred it round with a steel spoon.

'There's not much left of the factory?' I projected my remark towards the clergyman hoping to involve him in the conversation. He continued to gaze at the devastation. 'Not quite correct, mate,' the soldier chuckled and nodded toward the half-demolished Millenium Mill. 'There's bits of Brunner Mond in that lot. See that twisted metal in the side of the fifth storey ... well that's the boiler. The explosion lifted it a hundred feet and buried it in the side of the mill. Molten hot metal was showered on to the place and it just caught fire like it was dried grass. The men and women what worked there jumped out into the river to escape and some of 'em couldn't swim. It was either drown or burn for some of 'em. No 3 company Essex Regiment fished four out of river this morning.'

The fire was crackling and spitting as the damp wood burned. The soldier bent down and broke the remains of someone's upholstered armchair and threw it, a leg at a time, on to the fire.

The mill had burnt from the inside and its concrete walls remained standing like a cage on stilts. The firemen with attendant engines were pouring pumped river water into its remaining skeleton. A mournful column of smoke rose into the grey morning sky – like smoke signal conveying a terrible message. The silence was broken only by the throbbing of the fire pumps as they sucked the water from the river.

'Just like the Somme this is,' the soldier spat into the fire. 'Just like the Somme. Even that water

People returning to their homes were stunned and saddened by the destruction.

there. The Germans mined under the Welsh Regiment's trenches and blew 'em up with a mine. I saw it on my way to join the Border Regiment. They were all killed before I got there. Just like this. Quiet, very quiet. Bodies lay like broken birds, twisted and sprawling where they'd caught it.'

The clergyman turned and walked away towards the remains of the Sunday School chapel. 'He seems very shaken, doesn't he?' I handed my mug back to the soldier.

'Aye well, Mister – he's seen sights in the dawn that make any man sick in the stomach. A policeman picked up a torso without arms or legs and wheeled it in a barrow to the hospital – and he asked the vicar there to bless it and say a few words like. There was children and babies just burned alive and he and some woman worked all night trying to get the bricks off 'em. He found one of the firemen's daughters in a bit of garden at the back of her house. She'd been blown through the window and broke her back. He carried her to a mattress in the middle of the road and she died there. I've seen his look on the faces of many soldiers on the Somme. It's a look you don't see anywhere else.'

The soldier tapped his cup on a piece of wood and swilled out the tea-leaves with hot water from his billy can. Hitching his rifle on his back he prepared to move off. 'Must resume my patrol now, sir. Don't mention my name in the paper, sir, if you don't mind.'

'Why are you patrolling?'

'Pilfering and looting, sir. Caught two men just

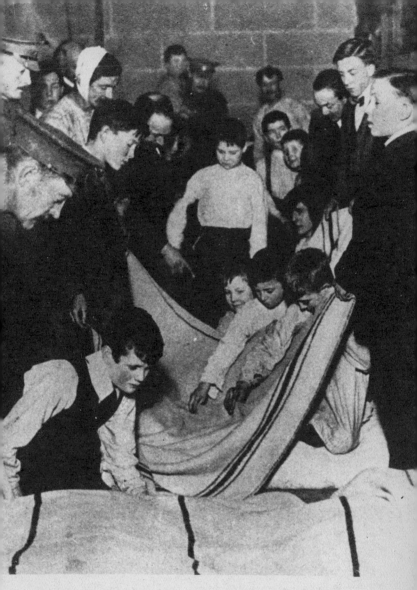

Some children from the 'Band of Hope' party slept in a
school for the night.

before midnight. They were looking for valuables. If I'd had a fixed bayonet I'd have run 'em through there and then.' He marched off briskly to resume his duties.

As I gazed about me and absorbed the scene of destruction I recalled the soldier's words – 'Just like the Somme, sir – Just like the Somme.'

Mena re-read the account as if she couldn't take it all in the first time. Jane sat back and stared vacantly at the library shelves. Reading about the effects of the explosion was very disturbing. In some peculiar way the information presented in the form of a newspaper made it more immediate. It didn't seem like sixty years ago. It was like reading of events which had happened last week.

Mena fingered the line describing the death of the fireman's daughter.

'That's the girl who wrote the diary, I'm sure. It doesn't mention her by name – but it's bound to be her.'

'I think you're right,' Jane said, 'but let's ask Mr Watkins, perhaps he's got some way of proving it.'

On request, Mr Watkins produced the coroner's reports from the inquests. It was a gruesome list.

The coroner then proceeded to take evidence of identification of the bodies.

The first witness was the licensee of a public house who identified the body of his manager, aged 36, who was found on the premises by the police.

A city fruit salesman identified the body of his grandfather, Mr Foster, aged 67.

A labourer living in Oldfield Street identified the body of his son, aged 8.

A labourer identified the bodies of his son and two daughters.

The body of a Liverpool plumber, aged 30, was identified by his landlady.

A lady who had her arm in a bandage said she was having her tea with her husband when they saw the light. He advised her to leave the house. She did so but her husband was buried in the debris of the house which collapsed, and the body was not recovered till the morning.

A mill hand, Mr Hopkins, of Oldfield Road, identified the body of his wife, age 32, which he saw in the mortuary. At another mortuary he recognised his son, aged 13, and his baby daughter of four months was found amongst the wreckage of his home.

Mr Ernest Parks, gas worker, identified his brother-in-law, Edgar Werborn, by recognising his foot by the boot and sock and from the fact that a piece of the Providential Almanac had been put in the boot to ease it.

Harold Dibbs, a clerk, identified Winifred Dibbs, his sister. At 7.30 he saw her being carried by

GALLANT FIREMEN KILLED AND INJURED IN THE GREAT EXPLOSION.

Sub-officer Vickers, dead

Fireman J. J. Betts, injured.

Fireman Chapple, injured.

Station Officer S. S. Betts (standing), injured, and Fireman Yabsley, seriously injured.

Fireman Dibbs, killed.

Fireman Dibbs's little daughter was also killed.

Some of the firemen who made every effort to subdue the fire which led to the great explosion.

a clergyman from a garden at the back of the fire station houses. He helped to lay her on a mattress by the pavement, and she died there.

The girls were shocked by the terrible price paid by poor Mr Hopkins. Mena's eyes stung with tears at the death of the new baby.

Jane re-read the brief description of Winnie's death a dozen times. It was an odd experience. They had set out to discover the *life* of a girl who lived over sixty years ago, and here they were faced with an account of her *death*.

The information seemed a perfect match, and the additional information about the Hopkins family confirmed what Mena had first thought. The girls could now say with reasonable certainty that Winifred Dibbs had died in the street attended by a clergyman and her brother. Despite the tragic nature of their discoveries the girls were strangely excited. In the space of two days they had seen into the life of Winnie Dibbs. The information came to them in patches.

'It's a bit like waiting for one of those polaroid camera photographs to develop,' Mena said.

Both girls were now firmly hooked on the project. They would find out all about Winnie Dibbs just because they wanted to know.

5

The two girls were now spending several hours each day after school researching in the Reference Library. Winnie was constantly in their minds, so it was perhaps not surprising that one of them should start to dream about her.

Jane told Mena about her dream, and Mena was very disturbed.

'How does she appear,' she inquired nervously.

'She was wearing a white dress, and she was playing in the street with lots of children – like in charge of them – organising them like a teacher.'

'What were they playing?' Mena asked, getting very agitated.

'Well, you know dreams ... it wasn't very clear what they were doing exactly, except at the end they sang *Ring a Ring of Roses*. Then everyone fell down and went to sleep. All except Winnie who walked into the house. She had a book under her arm.'

'Did she speak to you?'

'She told me she'd won the scholarship,' Jane smiled. 'But it's only a dream.'

'No it's not. It's not. It's very serious, Jane.' Mena was near to tears. 'We've disturbed her spirit. We shouldn't be doing this ... this project.'

'Disturbed her spirit? What the blazes are you talking about? She's dead and buried long ago.'

Jane had never seen Mena so upset.

'No, Jane. You don't understand. In our religion, when relatives die, we say goodbye in the gurdwara, and then we never mention them by name again. They are left to rest in peace. Perhaps you thought it odd that I have not mentioned our own friend's name since she died in the accident, but this is the reason. I haven't spoken the name of the Silvertown explosion girl, either, but you have, and Mr Watkins has. Perhaps because her name has been spoken and we have read her diary she is upset and she's telling us to stop it. She's a disturbed spirit making herself known in the only way she can ... in your dream.'

'You don't believe that, do you? I've dreamed about lots of people dead and alive and they've never complained. I just don't believe in that dream rubbish. It's like fortune-telling – a load of baloney.'

Mena sat down on the rustic seat by the rose bushes. Jane stood behind her, awkward and embarrassed. Mena began to sob. Jane lent her a handkerchief and patted her shoulder.

'Why do you take it so seriously? It's only a dream.'

Mena dried her eyes.

'You must try and understand, Jane. It's part of our religion. We believe the dead should be left alone to enjoy their eternal rest. We must stop our project. Anyway, the parts about ... about the girl, otherwise she will appear in your dreams forever.'

Jane was startled by the last statement. The idea of meeting Winnie every night for the next fifty years or so was not an inviting prospect. It wasn't that she didn't like Winnie, it was just that she preferred a certain variety in her dream encounters – an occasional visit from David Essex perhaps – to break the monotony.

'We can't jack in the project. What about Tracey? What about Mrs Thomas? That's one of the drawbacks of having the headmistress taking you for History. She wants proper reasons for throwing it in, does Madam. You can't fool her.'

'That is a proper reason,' Mena said.

Jane screwed up her eyes until the bushes went blurred and out of focus.

'Listen, Mena. There's a bit more. Just let me tell you. You see, in another part of the dream Wi . . . she came into this garden, here, picking roses and giving them to Billy Taplow. Mrs Thomas saw them and came towards them carrying a pile of our History notebooks. Instead of shouting at them, she plucked some roses herself and gave them to Winnie, and they all went off to a large building with corridors.'

At the mention of Winnie's name Mena grabbed Jane's arm.

'Promise me, promise me you won't say her name. Promise!'

Jane shook her off roughly.

'All right, all right. But it seems stupid to me.'

'It isn't stupid. It's very important for . . . the girl.'

'All right. But don't go on about it. And it won't be easy. We're bound to slip up now and then.'

'Did she say anything to you? Did she give you a message?' asked Mena.

'It's only a dream I had. It wasn't a

51

telephone call . . . from up there.' Jane indicated the heavens.

'Dreams can be very important,' Mena said seriously. 'In India the storytellers retell some of the oldest stories of the Punjab, and dreams play an important part in them. Sometimes the dreams warn of danger and at other times they are prophecies . . .'

Jane laughed.

'But those stories are for children. No grown-up person actually believes them. If I dream of David Essex in our school hall, he doesn't appear with Madam the following morning, does he? If I thought that was true, I'd be trying to dream of him every night.'

Mena was not amused.

'This is a trivial pop star. He is not important. If the girl in your dreams is upset we must do something. I will ask my mother this evening. She is very wise in these matters. I don't want to continue this conversation, Jane, because you might mention her name again. So excuse me. I'm going home.'

Mena got up and walked towards the school gate. Jane remained seated looking at the flowers, thinking.

'Well, Jane, you are very deep in thought. I hope nothing is wrong.'

It was Mrs Thomas. Jane stood up at once.

'It's all right, child. Sit down. Sit down.'

Mrs Thomas lowered herself on to the bench. Jane moved to the end of the seat to allow her the maximum space.

'I often come here myself for a few quiet moments. The creation of this garden was really a selfish idea of mine. It meant I always had a place where I could get away from the noise.'

She fingered a pale yellow blossom.

'Daffodils are such a complete and beautiful bloom. My late husband adored them. He always sent me spring flowers. I suppose that's why I grow them – to remind me.'

'You're a widow, then?' Jane blurted, before she could stop herself.

'Yes, Jane. I'm a widow. My husband was killed in the last war. He was a pilot in the Royal Air Force.'

'I'm sorry Madam,' Jane said, feeling uncomfortable.

'No need to be, my girl. It's twenty-eight years since he was shot down over Germany. We'd been married just seven months.'

'Do you dream about him?' Jane could have bitten her tongue off. She flushed crimson.

'Yes, from time to time, Jane. From time to

time. And I have one advantage over other women, Jane. My husband never ages. When I dream about him he's twenty-four, young, active and ...' She paused, smiled at Jane. 'That was a very interesting question, Jane. Why did you ask?'

'Because we've struck a snag in our project. You know its about ... about this girl in the Silvertown explosion. Mena says we've disturbed her eternal rest, and I'll probably dream about her now, forever.'

Jane explained the position. Mrs Thomas gazed into the distance. For a while Jane thought she was thinking about something else. Perhaps the problem was too small and too insignificant for a truly clever person like Madam.

'Listen, Jane,' she said, finally. 'I wouldn't like to say whether Mena is right or wrong. In any case, it isn't a question of right or wrong. Different religions have different customs and beliefs,and before we judge, we must try to understand. One thing is certain, though, and that is that because of these differences, dreams figure differently in different cultures and societies. For instance, I could say that your dream reflects some thinking you are doing – some unconscious thinking that you have put in your dream. Of course, it isn't all that clear yet what you are working out. Mena has grown up thinking about it in another way. She will certainly tell her mother what has happened, so let's wait until tomorrow, and see what Mrs Sandhu says. She is very wise in these things. She will know what to do.'

That evening after school Jane went to the library on her own. She told Mr Watkins that Mena wasn't feeling too well, and then she continued to search the contents of the brown cardboard boxes in which much of the Silvertown materials were stored. She came across the typewritten letter from the Ministry of Munitions to the Mayor of West Ham.

Dear Sir,

We are pleased to inform you that the King has graciously contributed £250 towards the relief of the sufferers in the recent explosion. £100 has also been received from Her Majesty the Queen and £100 from Her Majesty Queen Alexandra. The Princess Royal has sent a contribution of £50 and the bankers N M Rothschild & Sons have donated £105. The money is to be used in dealing with exceptional cases.

Pinned to it, with a rusty paper clip, was a yellowed cutting from a local newspaper.

Gallant Firemen's Funeral

Imposing Procession through the Borough

On Tuesday afternoon four of the victims of the recent explosion in a munitions factory in the East End were laid to rest in the Corporation cemetery.

The victims were all associated with the local fire brigade and two of them, Sub-Officer Vicars and Fireman Dibbs, were the gallant firemen who met their deaths when, with their colleagues, they were making arrangements to cope with the fire which produced the explosion. At the same time there were buried Winifred Dibbs, daughter of Fireman Dibbs, and the infant child of fireman Betts.

Every public honour was conferred upon them. The funeral procession met at the fire station in the southern part of the borough. The coffins, draped in union jacks and covered with a profusion of beautiful floral tribute, were borne to the cemetery on motor fire engines. Alongside the motor engines walked members of the Fire Brigade headed by Acting Superintendent Robinson.

The procession was headed by the band of 'K' division of the Metropolitan Police, and every department in public life in the Borough of West Ham was represented in the long procession which followed the coffins.

The day was bitterly cold and snow was falling during the greater part of the journey to the Parish

Church, but in spite of these discouraging weather conditions thousands of people lined the route and reverently paid their last respects to the gallant dead.

The band played the Dead March as the procession wound its way slowly through the town. Immediately behind the band came the two fire engines bearing the bodies of the firemen and then a private hearse containing the coffins of Winifred Dibbs and the small child.

The Mayor walked in his robes of office supported by large numbers of Council Members and officials of the Corporation. Alderman Mansfield, the Town Clerk (Mr GE Hilleard) and Alderman Will Thorne, MP, walked the whole distance from the fire station to the cemetery.

Winifred Dibbs was a scholarship holder at the West Park Central School and a number of her young friends were present at the church. They were accompanied by Dr Burness (Principal) and Miss Jeremy (Mistress of her form).

At the Parish Church the funeral cortege was met by the Bishop of Chelmsford, the Bishop of Barking and the Reverend Roger Travers (Vicar of the Borough).

A tear trickled down Jane's nose and dripped on to the back of her hand. This simple newspaper description took possession of her imagination. So Winnie had won her scholarship to the grammar school. She

57

pictured herself as Winnie's mother wearing a black coat and veil and walking desolate and alone through the streets lined with silent people. The mayor and the aldermen were walking by her side to support her. Alderman Thorne, MP, occasionally holding her arm in support.

Jane's sobs attracted the attention of Mr Watkins. He walked over, glanced at the newspaper cutting, and putting his arm round her shoulders, gave her a gentle hug.

'Look, Jane, I'm delighted that you and Mena have taken such a tremendous interest in Winnie, but I don't want you getting upset. War and its victims are not the happiest things for you to study. Perhaps you and Mena should give it all a rest for a week – think of something else – go to the cinema or the theatre – go out and enjoy yourselves.' He glanced at his watch. 'The library will be closing in ten minutes. Just tidy some of these papers and put them in their right boxes, then I'll give you a lift home in my car.'

Jane liked Mr Watkins' car. It was a Sierra, silver and blue with white trimming down each side. The front seats had head rests and the radio aerial was automatic. She listened to *Capitol Radio* as he drove through the streets –

the same streets through which Winifred's body had been carried.

After Mr Watkins had dropped her off at the corner of Ashcroft Street he turned off the radio. The girls' enthusiasm for the Silvertown project was now affecting him. He was wondering about Winnie. She did seem to appear regularly in the trail of events. How could he possibly track down more pages of the diary – presuming they existed – and did those letters she wrote to Alfie the boy in her class survive the explosion? He knew more than the girls about the death of Winnie's father, though. A local vicar who was a member of the Local Studies group had made some tape recordings in an Old Folks Home. Amongst them was a tape, recording the voice of Fireman Betts – aged 92. His voice was sharp and clear, and although he tended to repeat events, he was definite about the explosion.

'Fireman Yapton comes into the station running. "Fred, Fred," he shouts, "Brunner Mond's on fire – get all the help you can." My father was in charge that night. "Well, lads," he says, "you know the score. It could go up at any time, and us with it. Anybody what wants to pull out can do so, but I'm going now. A delay could *cost a life." 'Course nobody withdrew and he tells me to phone round for assistance. I picks up the phone and I get Balaam Street Station – they had a motorised engine – I says, "We need assistance. Brunner Mond's on fire ..." And then I remembers no more till I woke up in the hospital. My dad was recognisable when they found him but the gatemen just disappeared. They found Arthur Somerfield's watch and that was all. Three of 'em vanished like a conjuring trick at the theatre. Maggie Laurence – she were a one – a real rum girl. She worked in the hopper over the steam furnace. They found her finger with her wedding ring on. Quite a few people were just never seen again.'*

Mr Watkins closed his garage door. He made a note to listen to the vicar's tapes again. Perhaps he should circulate all the homes in the area asking for survivors – an advert in the paper? Why not? If he was supposed to bring local events to life, why not ask the living to leave behind a permanent record.

The following morning the borough librarian gave permission for an advert to be inserted in the local paper.

6

Mena's mother suggested that they call Winnie the Silvertown Girl. She said they could continue their research so long as they did not refer to the dead girl by name. It was the actual naming of a dead person that showed lack of respect. It was acceptable to refer to them in another way. Mena felt considerably relieved. It had felt very uncomfortable and unsettling to think she was going against the traditions of her religion.

Jane agreed to abide by Mrs Sandhu's suggestion.

'Does that mean that Wi ... er ... the Silvertown Girl's spirit won't be restless anymore?'

'No. My mother says that it doesn't mean that. Her spirit would be disturbed for other reasons – like things inside herself that worried her before she died. It's just that if we don't use her name we will not be responsible for her restlessness, not responsible for disturbing her peace.'

It was a Thursday evening, and although Mr Watkins was away at a Librarians' conference at Norwich, he had left some research work for Jane and Mena to complete. His own investigation had revealed a description of the way TNT at the Brunner Mond factory was purified. He had asked the two girls to read the description and draw a diagram of the process.

Art was one of Jane's strong points so she drew the sketch while Mena sorted out details of the process and made a fair copy of their notes.

They discovered that the crude TNT was placed in a container which, in turn, was placed over a boiler. The TNT was purified by boiling it in a vacuum with heated alcohol. Then it was rolled out on cold rollers, after which the workers – all women, because most of the men were away at the war – flaked off the TNT with wooden spades.

To work with TNT in this way was very dangerous but, because the generals were continually needing more shells to fight the war in France, the risk to people's lives at home was one the government were prepared to take.

'I wonder if they fully realised what they were doing?' Mena said.

'Who?' Jane was sucking the end of her pencil, and gazing expertly at her drawing.

'The girls – the people who worked there.'

'I don't understand, Mena. What are you gassing about?'

'Well, these people, these sixty-three people who worked on this process, they produced TNT for shells which in a week or two would very likely kill a lot of men. It was a kind of death factory. I mean, if you worked next door at the flour mill you made bread. If you worked at Brunner Mond you produced explosives for killing soldiers.'

Jane considered the idea as she put the finishing touches to her drawing. 'They were at war with Germany,' she said. 'If they didn't kill 'em and win the war where would we be? We'd all be Germans now. You'd be Fraulein Mena Schmidt and I'd be Fraulein Jane Schnell. If you're in a war, you've got to win. You've got to kill.'

'Mahatma Gandhi said all wars are futile. Man killing man for any reason is wrong.'

Mena was strangely intent as she said this. Her father and mother had been talking about Gandhi two nights previously, and she had been very impressed by his simple message. It was made more obvious to her by the news on television that night which showed men being killed in Northern Ireland, Iran and India.

'People are still killing each other today,' Mena continued, 'and everyone suffers – just like these people in Silvertown. Sixty-nine people killed on the spot – 4 died later, and 98 seriously injured. It's a lot of people, and they had nothing to do with the war. The government might have thought it was a risk worth taking, but what about the people? Do you think our Silvertown Girl agreed with it?'

Jane couldn't answer, but all the way home her imagination was filled with thoughts of the dead girl of sixty or so years ago.

That night, Jane dreamed about Winnie. In the dream, a large exercise book lay open on Mrs Thomas's desk. It was covered in red leather. On the outside, in red letters, it said *War Book*. Inside were lists of people who were killed. Jane started to draw one of those big guns with the wheels on each side, and before she could finish it, out of nowhere, a soldier rushed forward, put a shell in it and fired it. The shell was clearly marked in white, *Made in Silvertown*. The shell landed in the school, and destroyed the garden and collapsed the front of the school. Everyone seemed to be eating school dinners. Mrs Thomas staggered out of the garden obviously injured. A man in an RAF uniform and Winnie were helping her. Winnie was wearing her white frock. The dinner ladies were looking after everyone like nurses, and Winnie came up to Jane and took her pencil. In slow handwriting she put a message on Jane's book. It read, *Tell Billy Taplow to bring flowers tomorrow*. Then she gave Jane the pencil. Immediately, it sprouted a rose. Jane bent down to smell the rose. She remembered the question about whether Winnie agreed with the war, but Winnie had gone into a house carrying a book. Jane turned to follow her, and woke up.

Jane had her project work on a table in her bedroom. She got out of bed, found some paper in her project folder, and wrote down everything she could remember. She was very excited. She could not write fast enough, and what was she to make of it all? *Tell Billy Taplow to bring flowers tomorrow*. The message was clear enough, but what had Billy Taplow to do with Winifred Dibbs? Jane did not think much of Billy Taplow. She thought he was stupid, ignorant and daft, because he was always getting into trouble, being picked up by the police. The girl at the Old Folks Home must be a raving lunatic to go out with him. Still, in the dream, Winnie did not find him objectionable.

The following afternoon, Jane sat in the school garden and waited. At about four o'clock Billy appeared at the school gate. He looked around, and when he was sure it was safe he strolled casually towards the daffodils. From his pocket he produced a pair of household scissors. He snipped a bloom from two or three clusters and was about to snip a fourth when he saw Jane.

'Don't mind me, Billie. Carry on. I'm sure your lady friend will like them very much.'

Billy was dumbfounded. Normally when he was caught doing something wrong people scolded him. Jane's smile was very unsettling. It just wasn't right. He stood there uncertain what to do.

'How many flowers do you normally pinch, Billy?'

'Oh . . . about half a dozen . . . well, perhaps, five . . . depends.'

He held the flowers in his hand as if he'd put them back if he could.

'You're a couple short, then,' she said, walking forward, taking the scissors out of his hand and cutting two more blooms. She put them to her nose. 'Lovely, Billy. You have a smell.'

She thrust them under his nose and he backed away.

'Come on,' she said. 'Put them with the rest, then we can get going.'

'Going?' He looked startled and afraid. 'You're not going to shop me, are you?'

'No, I'm coming to meet your girlfriend at the Home. Unless you *want* me to shop you, of course.'

Billy turned quickly and without waiting for Jane walked through the school gate. This suited Jane well. She didn't want to be seen walking side by side with Billy Taplow. People might jump to the wrong conclusions. It was all right for Winnie to walk with him in her dreams because no one except Jane could see her doing it.

Jane trailed behind him down the street. He was walking quite quickly, and occasionally turned round to see if she was following him.

Turning left, he crossed the road by the Parish Church and walked a hundred yards down Robins Lane. The Home was on the right-hand side. He stopped at the gates, glancing quickly to see if she was following, and went in.

He made his way to the back door and knocked.

'He's brought you your daily bunch of daffs,' Jane said to the young woman who opened the door.

'Oh, good. I love daffs, and so do the ladies and gentlemen in the wards. Would you like to come in and help him put them in a jar of water?'

Jane was puzzled by the young woman attitude, but she accepted the invitation and entered the clean, white-tiled kitchen. The woman brought a vase filled with water, and they arranged the flowers in it. Billy stood a yard away watching.

'Now, Billy,' the woman said, 'off you go and do your good deed for the day. You go with him, love.'

Billy carried the vase of daffodils into a corridor which had glass walls and was divided into small compartments. Each compartment contained a bed and chair and a patient. They were all very old. Most of them were asleep. Billy selected a lady who was wide awake and sitting up in bed doing some knitting.

'Hello, Louise,' he called, placing the flowers on a locker beside her bed. 'It's your turn today.'

'Well, well, well, me boy,' she said, smiling. 'What a lovely surprise.' She smelled the

68

daffodils. 'Lovely flowers. Remind me of my garden at home in Lancashire.' She turned to Jane. 'Not always lived down here, you know. I used to live in Clitheroe in Lancashire. Beautiful town right near the countryside. How old do you think I am, dearie?'

Jane was taken by surprise with this question. She looked at Billy for help. He moved behind her shoulder and mouthed the words '61'.

'Sixty-one,' Jane said, with authority.

The old lady cackled and shook her head.

'Sixty-one? Sixty-one? Good God, girl, I'm nearly eighty-two.'

Jane looked across at Billy, and gave him a petrifying look. He pretended not to notice.

'I was sixteen when I came to London, my girl. I left my family in Clitheroe – well, family isn't quite right – I was brought up by an aunt – my Aunty Maud. Maud Williamson – everybody knew her because she had a newspaper and tobacconist's shop and she was famous for her canaries. She bred canaries that were national champions. She'd sell 'em for a pound a piece sometimes. Her canaries were famous – they used 'em down the pits when there was gas about. If the canary died when they lowered it down the shaft, the miners knew there was dangerous gas about.'

The old lady gabbled on, encouraged by Billy, who stood at the bottom of the bed giggling and nodding his head. Jane felt a peculiar cold, prickly feeling spreading up her spine and ending at the back of her neck. Her hair seemed to stiffen. She remembered Winnie's letter which described how her sister Lucy had rented a house while her husband had gone to the war, and how they had returned from America and brought enough money with them to pay a year's rent. She remembered that two girls had lodged with Lucy and that one had been called Louise – Louise who told funny stories about her aunt in Lancashire who bred canaries. The coincidence was frightening.

Tell Billy Taplow to bring the flowers, Winnie had said in Jane's dream, and Jane had made sure that he had done so. By this lucky chance she had been led straight to Louise. If she went on like this, she would start to believe that dreams came true.

Jane stared at the old lady.

'Louise, did you once use to work at the Brunner Mond factory? In 1917? When there was the big explosion?'

'Yes. I was there at the time of the explosion, love. So was Mary, over there.'

70

Louise pointed at another old woman, fast asleep in an opposite cubicle. 'We both was in the explosion.'

Jane turned quickly and ran down the corridor and out into the drive. She was running not really knowing where to go. She was very frightened. She ran back towards school. As she came level with the gate, she saw Mrs Thomas getting into her car. Jane ran straight for her, and flung her arms round her.

'Madam! Madam! I've had a dream, and it's come true. I've found them, just like Winnie said.'

Jane burst into a fit of sobbing which took Mrs Thomas a full five minutes to stop. Then she took Jane back into school to her study, made her a cup of tea, and got her to explain the whole thing.

7

Mrs Thomas was very interested in Jane's story. The following day, she rang the matron of the Home and got permission to visit the two sisters. She asked Mr Harding to prepare a tape recorder with a good microphone. Then, she, Jane, Mena and Mr Harding all piled into Mr Harding's car and drove round to the Home.

Miss Ransome, the nurse that Jane had mistaken for Billy's girlfriend, greeted them at the door. Matron was there, too, to make sure that everything was done correctly, and that her patients did not get too tired or over excited.

'Welcome to Walsingham,' she said. 'The ladies are looking forward to your visit, but I hope you can keep the excitement to a minimum. At their age one never knows, does one?'

'We'll be as discreet as possible,' Mrs Thomas told her, 'but this is an exciting day for these girls, too. They might even be more anxious than Louise and Mary.'

'Just as long as we understand each other,' Matron said, showing them into the lounge where the two sisters were seated, in two armchairs.

Louise got up immediately and shook hands with everybody.

'How old do you think I am?' she asked.

They all guessed in turn and Jane said sixty-one again. All the wrong answers delighted Louise.

'I'm eighty-two – eighty-two and three months to be exact. I've not always lived here you know. I was born in Lancashire . . .'

The nurse took her gently by the hand and led her back to the chair. Jane wondered whether old people's conversation was always like a record that got stuck in a groove, repeating over and over again.

Mary sat quietly, and smiled at everyone.

Mr Harding set up the microphone on a stand in between the chairs. After a few test runs, he announced he was ready to record. Mrs Thomas began the questions, by asking how old they were, and Louise told her story about her aunt and the canaries again. Then Mrs Thomas handed over the questioning to Mena, who explained what she and Jane were doing. When she asked them about the explosion, Louise and Mary really got into their stride.

Louise began the story.

'Well, dearie, it was like this. Mary and me shared the same lodgings in Oldfield Road and we worked in the kitchens of the factory – doing the meals for the shift workers. We was getting ready to go home – it would be about five minutes to seven – when there's this bloody great bang. Sorry about the swear word, I forgot you was recording. Now, where was I, Mary?'

Mary stirred herself, and replied in a high squeaky voice. 'We'd just heard a bloody great bang.'

'Correct,' Louise said. "Correct. Well, a ball of fire shot through the air and landed in the canteen. People escaped by leaping through windows into the river. Some of 'em couldn't swim, so I heard. There were three explosions, and the buildings fell about us like a pack of cards. Lots of women were killed on the spot. I was knocked unconscious, wasn't I, Mary?'

Mary responded.

'Yes, Louise, you were. You were knocked unconscious. It was nearly nine o'clock when we got out. Two hours we were. Two hours.'

'We were trapped you see,' Louise continued. 'My other mate, Helen – well Nellie we called her – she had beautiful hair. I can see it now. It was so long she could sit on it. Well she was standing next to me when it happened.' Louise paused, dabbed her nose with her handkerchief and continued. 'An iron bar fell on us. I was lucky because I fell between two cookers – and when I looked up, she was dead. She didn't suffer at all. It was very quick. One moment she was there – next thing she was in paradise. This iron bar caught her across her neck. Her hair didn't have a single strand out of place.'

'She was lovely,' Mary added, smiling.

'She was very beautiful, even in death. It was all very strange. There was all that noise, and then, no noise at all. Just an occasional dripping sound. The silence was almost as frightening as the explosion. I could hear someone breathing, very gently, breathing in and out, in and out, then after a few minutes, it stopped. Just silence, then – and this dripping sound.'

Mr Harding's mouth was wide open as he listened totally engrossed in the story.

'What happened then?' he asked.

Louise took up the story again.

'Well, we waited, but nobody came. I

suppose they were too busy. Our part of the factory wasn't the one that had gone up. I suppose they didn't think to look in our direction. So I says to Mary, come on, gal, this won't do. We'll have to help ourselves.'

Louise stood up, and disregarding the microphone, began to show them just how it had happened.

'We started to feel around. We had to be very careful. One wrong move and it might all come down on top of us. I cottons on to a big metal beam. So I says to Mary, come on, gal. We'll lift this and see what happens.'

'That's quite right,' Mary piped. 'We had to be very careful, though. I cut myself on the jagged edges in several places. Didn't I, Louise?'

'Yes, you did, gal. Well, anyway, we lifts a bit and there's a God Almighty clattering of wreckage, but it did the trick. We sees a bit of light, and we starts to slide on our bottom underneath the kitchen tables.'

'It got a bit lighter – probably from all the fires around – they were still burning away, weren't they, Louise?'

'Yes, yes, they were that. Anyway, we reaches the outside – well it was a window, actually, on the top floor. So I looks out, and

76

it's one hell of a drop. Then I sees this piece of guttering. So we edges along this guttering, clutching it with our hands. You daren't look down.'

Louise stretched up her arms and recreated the scene for everybody.

'She's much stronger than me,' Mary muttered. I couldn't hold it much longer, could I, Louise?'

'No gal, you couldn't. "You've got to hold on," I shouts at her. "I can't. I can't," she says. "Oh God, Louise, I'm going to fall," but I grasps her wrist to give her confidence and we waits till she can grab another piece of guttering sticking out of the wall. So we climbs down. Didn't we, gal?'

Louise sat down exhausted.

'We fell down more like, Louise.' Mary said, taking up the story. 'We had a bit of a rest, and still nobody came. So we thought we'd better make our way out. We began walking towards Canning Town. That's when we started meeting people. They were all walking very slowly. Just like us. Some were carrying children – only stretcher cases got any help – we were the walking wounded. I took off my petticoat, and wound it round my hand and my arm. When I got home I was taken to a friend who was a nurse – she took me straight to hospital. There was this old lady in the next bed who watched 'em bring me in, and settle me down. When they'd finished, she looked across and said, "You're not as bad as me, love", and then she died.'

Mary paused for a moment. Her eyes gazed out through the window into the garden beyond. She was remembering the events now very clearly. She returned to her armchair, and Mr Harding made her comfortable by arranging her cushion.

'What about Winnie?' It was the first time Jane had spoken. 'Did you know a young girl called Winnie? She was killed in the explosion and buried with the firemen.'

The mention of the Silvertown Girl by name brought back all Mena's discomfort. She wished Jane could have been more careful but, even as she thought that, she realised that this time Jane had no choice. The old ladies would not have known who they were talking about otherwise.

Mary answered at once.

'Oh, yes,' Mary said. 'She was our landlady's younger sister. She came to the house now and then when we were there. She was a nice girl. Very quiet. Very thoughtful. Of course, she was very clever. She won a scholarship at thirteen. She was rather lonely, I used to think. Always playing with the younger children. Organised games for them in the street. Seen her many a time playing singing games and *Ring a Ring of Roses*, and things like that. You knew her, too, didn't you, Louise?'

Mary turned to look at her sister. Louise had fallen asleep.

'Winnie Dibbs!' Mary shouted. 'You knew Winnie Dibbs, didn't you, Louise?'

Louise continued to snooze. Mena intervened.

'Did she write a lot?' she asked.

Mary chuckled.

'Oh yes, she wrote letters to everybody. She'd sooner leave a note than talk to you. I remember we all had a giggle when she wrote letters to that Alfie in Custom House. Alfie Needham. Poor fella, he died last week. He passed over very quietly.'

'You mean you knew him recently?' Mrs Thomas interjected.

'He was in here. In the next ward. We often talked about the old days. He died last week. It's his funeral tomorrow, isn't it, Matron?'

Matron nodded.

'Yes, poor man died of pneumonia. We did

our best. We've traced the relatives. They all live abroad except a daughter who is coming down to bury him. She lives in Glasgow.'

'Yes, got about a bit, did Alfie,' Louise said, waking up suddenly. 'In the Merchant Navy. Sailed the world, he did – still kept his seaman's chest. Wouldn't let anyone near it. We used to pull his leg, and say he was hiding the crown jewels. Didn't have much, I reckon. Nobody visited him except this daughter from Glasgow. Couple a times a year, that's all.'

Louise yawned and stood up, getting ready to dismiss them all.

'Well thanks very much, got to get my cup of tea and biscuits. Now, come on, Mary.'

They both got up abruptly as a bell rang for tea. They walked out arm in arm, leaving the two girls and their teachers staring after them in surprise. Matron chuckled.

'You must forgive those two. They're real characters. They live what's left of their lives according to their own rules – and who's to blame them? They enjoy it here, but they get tired quickly.'

'I want to look in Mr Needham's trunk,' Jane announced, feeling that the conversation was turning away from their real purpose.

'You can't look into the private effects of

the deceased,' Matron said, coldly. 'It's illegal.'

Jane was about to answer back, but Mrs Thomas intervened.

'I'll contact his daughter when she arrives from Glasgow. Is she staying here overnight, Matron?'

'She is. We have special accommodation for relatives if they have travelled some distance. She'll be here tomorrow morning.'

'Good. Then I'll give her a ring, and see if she is willing to speak to us. And, thank you, Matron, on behalf of all of us – especially these hardworking girls. They're like detectives on the hunt for the culprit – only this time, of course, it's not a criminal, it's the Silvertown Girl and her story.' She turned to Mr Harding and the girls. 'Come on, everyone, we had better take the tape to Mr Watkins. He'll be more than pleased, I'm sure.'

The excited group filled Mr Watkin's office. He was delighted, and pleased with the girls and with the prospect of both Mrs Thomas and Mr Harding joining in the research.

'It's becoming a co-operative venture now,' he said, grinning boyishly. 'When it's all put together it should be a fine piece of work.'

'Not until we get the letters,' Mena said. 'With the letters our project will be complete.'

'I'll bet his daughter won't let us look in his trunk,' Jane said, truculently. 'And if she does, I'll bet he's thrown them all away on his voyages abroad. Men do that when they meet other women. They burn all their letters so that their other girlfriends don't know.'

Mr Watkins did not give anyone time to pursue this line of conversation. He produced two envelopes from a drawer.

'These came yesterday,' he said. 'In response to the advert I placed in the local paper. They're not terribly relevant, but they're interesting enough for themselves.'

He opened one letter, and read it aloud.

Dear Sir,

I was a child at the time of the explosion. We lived in Custom House at the time. All my brothers had gone to bed and I walked to the corner shop for a loaf of bread. This big explosion happened and a huge gust of wind blew me off my feet. It was all quiet for a second, and then there was an almighty creaking and rumbling and half the street fell in. I don't remember much more except a man took my hand and we walked to Forest Gate, and a lady there gave us a cup of tea. I lost everybody, of course, and I was brought up by my uncle in Bow.

      Yours faithfully,
      Jimmy Edgar

P.S. I remember Mr Harlow who delivered salt, tea and provisions in Custom House. He was killed and his horse found its own way home to Jedson Road, Forest Gate. He was identified by the marriage licence in his pocket.

The second letter was quite different.

Dear Sir,

I see from the *Stratford Gazette* – which I picked up when passing through your area – that you are seeking information about the Silvertown disaster of 1917. *Have you nothing better to do? Librarians are paid to look after books* not nose around in the vile filth and violence of wars. The world is already full of violence without you collecting more of it. I suppose you intend writing one of these crude articles for the Sunday papers full of the nasty side of things. You ought to be ashamed. Just get on with the job you're paid to do.

> Yours in disgust,
> Concerned
> (Chislehurst)

Jane bridled as Mr Watkins read the letter.

'Cheeky sod! If he'd put his address on, I'd have told Billy Taplow. He'd have fixed him for you, Mr Watkins.'

Mrs Thomas smiled to herself. Jane had a happy knack of expressing everyone's feelings.

8

Mr Harding took Mrs Thomas and the two girls to Alfie Needham's funeral. Billy Taplow turned up at the cemetery, and Matron and a nurse represented the Home. Alfie's daughter, Mrs Didmarsh, was his only mourner.

There were three wreaths of flowers. One from his daughter, one from the Home, and one from Mrs Thomas and the girls. It was very sad when the coffin was lowered into the grave, and Mrs Didmarsh cried a little. At the end of the graveside prayers, Billy walked forward and placed a bunch of daffodils at the graveside. Jane could not help wondering which part of the garden he had nicked them from.

At four o'clock that afternoon, Mena and Jane went to Mrs Thomas's room. Mrs Didmarsh was there having a cup of tea, but more importantly, there was a small packet of documents tied with a red ribbon on Mrs Thomas's desk. Their headmistress indicated that they should sit down.

'Well, girls,' she began, 'I thought you'd like to open this to see if your letters – I mean – if the Silvertown Girl's letters are here.'

She passed the document to Mena who undid the ribbon. There was a legal document concerning a house, a will, some old bills, a war service card, two ribbons without their war medals, and a number of cigarette cards depicting wild flowers. There were no letters.

Jane could not disguise her disappointment.

'He's burned them, like I said. We'll never get to the bottom of this thing now.'

Mrs Thomas felt disappointed, too, and so did Mena. Mrs Didmarsh could see it, and was touched by the interest these total strangers were taking in her father.

'Perhaps there's something in the will,' she said.

Mrs Didmarsh took the will, unfolded it, and read it. The girls watched her face to see if it sparked with the light of discovery. It didn't. Mrs Didmarsh shook her head.

'Nothing here. He leaves all his money and effects, and that's not much, to me and I'm to sell the house. There's nothing here to help you girls, I'm afraid.'

It was while Mrs Thomas was thanking Mrs Didmarsh that Mena had a brainwave.

'Madam,' she said, 'could we please look through Mr Needham's house? Perhaps he's got some old letters there.'

'No, no, my girl. You can't ask Mrs Didmarsh to allow the house to be searched – that's an invasion of privacy. You shouldn't ask such a thing.'

'Oh, it's all right, Mrs Thomas. I don't mind. What the girls are doing seems right. I wish I'd had the chance to do such interesting work when I was at school. In any case, it will be like a memorial to my father, like it is for their own dead friend. I've got to go and look at the house tomorrow before I put it in the hands of an estate agent. I'd like the girls to come. It will be company for me, too.'

Immediately after school, Jane and Mena went to the library and told Mr Watkins. He acted at once, ringing Mrs Didmarsh to ask if he might come the next day to the house with the girls. She agreed.

It was a terraced house in Radcliffe Road, near the railway station. The front door opened onto a small hallway from which the stairs went up to the bedrooms. There was a front room, a back room, and a small kitchen. There were no carpets or curtains, and everything was covered in a layer of dirt and grime. Mr Needham had been in Walsingham Home for three years, and nobody had been near the house since. There were several dilapidated cane chairs, and a chest of drawers in the front room. The back room was absolutely bare. Some of the floorboards were rotting in places, and you could see down between them.

Jane went immediately to the chest of drawers. She searched each drawer as though she was looking for gold. There was nothing there. Under Mr Watkins's instructions, they pulled the drawers right out in case a letter had got stuck between the shelves. The chest was empty.

'Now, let's just pause and think about this, girls. If you were living here and you had some letters you wanted to keep, where would you put them?'

'I've got a private drawer I can lock in my bedroom,' Mena replied. 'But perhaps with men it's different.'

'I know a chap who hides bottles of whisky in the toilet,' Jane said unhelpfully, 'and his wife keeps finding 'em.'

Mr Watkins intervened before things got out of hand.

'Let's try the bedroom then, Mena. I'll go first, in case the wood in the stairs isn't safe.'

The front bedroom contained a double bed, a mattress and an oak wardrobe. Mr Watkins opened the wardrobe and looked inside. It was empty, except for a book on the shelf inside. He reached in and pulled it out. He blew the dust off it. It was a bible. The names of Alfie's children and his wife had been written inside the cover with the dates of their christenings. There was also a wedding photograph, brown and stained. In the photograph Alfie was wearing a navy uniform. His bride was in white, holding a posy of flowers. He flicked through the pages, and from the back cover a letter fell to the floor.

Mena and Jane stared at it as it lay there. The ink on the envelope had faded, and was now a purple colour. The handwriting was unmistakably that of the Silvertown Girl.

Mr Watkins reached down, and carefully – very carefully, for it would be very fragile after all these years – picked it up. Taking a nail file from his pocket he inched open the envelope, and levered out the letter. He put it on the mattress and smoothed it out so that they could all read it.

7 Oldfield Rd
January 8th 1917

No. 23

Dear Alfie,
this is my twenty-third
letter. I hope you keep them and turn
them into a book!
I'm still feeling very depressed.
Another Xmas has gone and the war
is still going on. There seems to be
no end to it. The list of the dead in
the 'Stratford Park Express' was
longer than ever. Twenty and thirty
soldiers are reported killed every week.
We're surrounded by it all. The Zeppelin
raids killed my mum's cousin last week
in Poplar and this factory - which I hate -
just carries on making dynamite for
shells. I just know something dreadful
is going to happen. I heard my father
talking to another fireman, and he
said that if Brunner Mond caught fire
there'd be no hope for anyone.
But what makes me really miserable
is that I read yesterday in a book in

89

the school library that 'Ring a Ring of Roses'
is a little story about the plague - the
Black Death. The roses are the marks
that appeared on people's arms when
they were about to catch it, and the
posies were bunches of herbs that
people carried to ward off the disease.
All fall down means they died. Well I
know, Alfie, for sure, this Brunner Mond
will blow up, and we'll all fall down.

Heres a poem for you

Skipping Poem by Winnie Dibbs

Poor Winnie shes a grieving - a grieving -
a grieving,
Poor Winnie shes a grieving on a cold
winter's day.
She wrote a little letter, a letter, a letter
To tell what she was thinking on a cold
winter's day.
But nobody was listening, was listening,
was listening,
But nobody was listening to what
she did say.

I'll write next week as usual
Winnie

The girls sighed both with satisfaction and sadness. They had found what they had been looking for – The Silvertown Girl – and understood her in her sadness and desolation.

9

Jane and Mena finished their project the day before they had to hand it in. It was in three parts, a folder, a tape-slide programme, and a play. They had marked the work clearly with their names so that the examiners could see who had done what, when they had worked separately and when they had written up things or created things together.

Mrs Thomas had helped them with a difficult, and – so the girls thought – silly task. They'd done the work together, so why shouldn't they be marked together. Certainly, as Mrs Thomas knew, the value and quality of the work owed everything to their collaboration and their joint commitment.

The folder contained their research materials, to which, lately, they had added a map of the area which showed the shock waves of the explosion, and a diagram which showed how the blast from Brunner Mond had zig-zagged across the area and missed some houses and factories. The folder also contained their account of the story.

Mr Watkins had helped them by photocopying the key documents for their folder and by lending them slides he had made of newspaper photographs of the destruction created by the explosion. With these slides, the tape-recording they had made, and their own scripted commentary Mena and Jane had made up a tape-slide programme called *The Silvertown Disaster*.

The play, which they had written and which they learned by heart so they could act it out, was the story Louise and Mary had told them. They called that *Explosion and Escape from the Works Canteen*.

In a way, Mena and Jane did not need the examiners and the marks they were going to get. They knew they had done a good piece of work. They also knew that they could not have made a better memorial both to their own friend and to the friend conjured up and made through history. To mark this they had written on the first page of the folder this simple message: *In memory of two dear friends*.

A copy was made for the library. Mrs Thomas keeps the original, and frequently refers to it when taking her History class as 'The Memorial'.

Knockouts
Founder Editor: Josie Levine

The Salmon   Ewart Alexander
Mia   Gunnel Beckman
Mia Alone   Gunnel Beckman
*The Marco File   Peter Buchanan
The Cat People   Jan Carew
Dark Night, Deep Water   Jan Carew
**Don't Go Near The Water*   Jan Carew
The Man Who Came Back   Jan Carew
**Dead Man's Creek*   Jan Carew
*House of Fear   Jan Carew
**Save The Last Dance For Me and other Stories*   Jan Carew
**Stranger Than Tomorrow*   Jan Carew
The Bike Racers   Bruce Carter
In the Beginning   John Christopher
Three Plays   Isobel D'Arcy
Twist of the Knife   Terry Deary
Walking Shadows   Terry Deary
Love at a Bus Stop   Janet Green
*The Six   Janet Green
Behind the Goal   John Griffin
A Person of Bad Character   John Griffin
All Creatures Great and Small   James Herriott
Vet in a Spin   James Herriott
Rumble Fish   S.E. Hinton
Week Out   Geraldine Kaye
**A Northern Childhood: The Balaclava Story and other Stories*
    George Layton
**A Northern Childhood: The Fib and other Stories*
    George Layton
A Taste of Freedom   Julius Lester
**Long Journey Home*   Julius Lester
Accident   Margaret Loxton
The Job   Margaret Loxton
The Sheene Machine   Andrew Marriott
It's Only Rock 'n' Roll   Alan McLean
Hostages   Kenneth McLeish
The Silvertown Disaster   Gerard Melia
Will of Iron   Gerard Melia
Fair Fight   Barry Pointon
Waves   David Rees
Evacuees   Ian Rodger
**The Bakerloo Flea*   Michael Rosen
**Nasty!*   Michael Rosen

94